Jasper M...

STEINER

ASSAULT ON THE

FRIENDLY
FIENDS

CUSTOMER SERVICE EXCELLENCE

Libraries & Archives

Kent
County
Council

Other books in the series:

DINOSAUR COVE™

ASSAULT OF THE FRIENDLY FIENDS

by
REX STONE

illustrated by
MIKE SPOOR

Series created by
Working Partners Ltd

OXFORD
UNIVERSITY PRESS

Special thanks to Jan Burchett and Sara Vogler

For Sara O'Connor and everyone at Working Partners — R.S.

These illustrations are dedicated to Sophie Butcher, Librarian, whose support for Dinosaur Cove is much appreciated — M.S.

OXFORD
UNIVERSITY PRESS

Great Clarendon Street, Oxford OX2 6DP

Oxford University Press is a department of the University of Oxford. It furthers the University's objective of excellence in research, scholarship, and education by publishing worldwide in

Oxford   New York

Auckland Cape Town Dar es Salaam Hong Kong Karachi
Kuala Lumpur Madrid Melbourne Mexico City Nairobi
New Delhi Shanghai Taipei Toronto

With offices in

Argentina Austria Brazil Chile Czech Republic France Greece
Guatemala Hungary Italy Japan Poland Portugal Singapore
South Korea Switzerland Thailand Turkey Ukraine Vietnam

Oxford is a registered trade mark of Oxford University Press
in the UK and in certain other countries

Series created by Working Partners Ltd
Dinosaur Cove is a registered trademark of Working Partners Ltd

The moral rights of the author have been asserted

Database right Oxford University Press (maker)

First published 2009

British Library Cataloguing in Publication Data

Data available

ISBN: 978-0-19-272897-5

1 3 5 7 9 10 8 6 4 2

Printed in Great Britain by CPI Cox and Wyman, Reading, Berkshire
Paper used in the production of this book is a natural, recyclable product made from wood grown in sustainable forests
The manufacturing process conforms to the environmental regulations of the country of origin

FACT FILE

➡️ JAMIE HAS JUST MOVED FROM THE CITY TO LIVE IN THE LIGHTHOUSE IN DINOSAUR COVE. JAMIE'S DAD IS OPENING A DINOSAUR MUSEUM ON THE BOTTOM FLOOR OF THE LIGHTHOUSE. WHEN JAMIE GOES HUNTING FOR FOSSILS IN THE CRUMBLING CLIFFS ON THE BEACH HE MEETS A LOCAL BOY, TOM, AND THE TWO DISCOVER AN AMAZING SECRET: A WORLD WITH REAL, LIVE DINOSAURS! BUT THE JURASSIC AGE CAN BE A VERY UNPREDICTABLE PLACE!

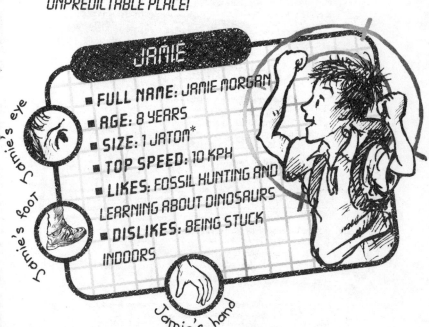

JAMIE

- **FULL NAME:** JAMIE MORGAN
- **AGE:** 8 YEARS
- **SIZE:** 1 JATOM*
- **TOP SPEED:** 10 KPH
- **LIKES:** FOSSIL HUNTING AND LEARNING ABOUT DINOSAURS
- **DISLIKES:** BEING STUCK INDOORS

Jamie's eye

Jamie's foot

Jamie's hand

*NOTE: A JATOM IS THE SIZE OF JAMIE OR TOM: 125 CM TALL AND 27 KG IN WEIGHT

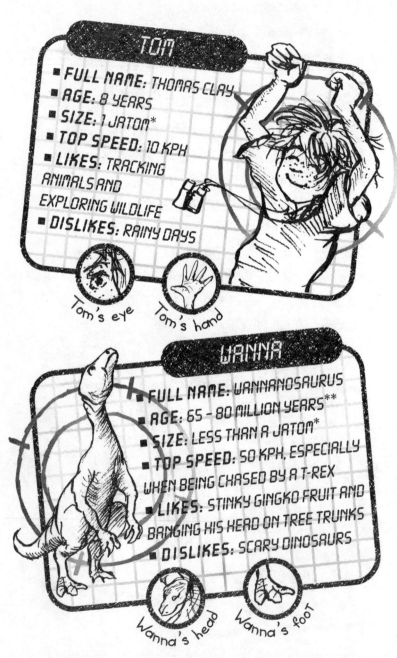

TOM

- **FULL NAME:** THOMAS CLAY
- **AGE:** 8 YEARS
- **SIZE:** 1 JATOM*
- **TOP SPEED:** 10 KPH
- **LIKES:** TRACKING ANIMALS AND EXPLORING WILDLIFE
- **DISLIKES:** RAINY DAYS

Tom's eye Tom's hand

WANNA

- **FULL NAME:** WANNANOSAURUS
- **AGE:** 65 – 80 MILLION YEARS**
- **SIZE:** LESS THAN A JATOM*
- **TOP SPEED:** 50 KPH, ESPECIALLY WHEN BEING CHASED BY A T-REX
- **LIKES:** STINKY GINGKO FRUIT AND BANGING HIS HEAD ON TREE TRUNKS
- **DISLIKES:** SCARY DINOSAURS

Wanna's head Wanna's foot

*NOTE: A JATOM IS THE SIZE OF JAMIE OR TOM: 125 CM TALL AND 27 KG IN WEIGHT
**NOTE: SCIENTISTS CALL THIS PERIOD THE LATE CRETACEOUS

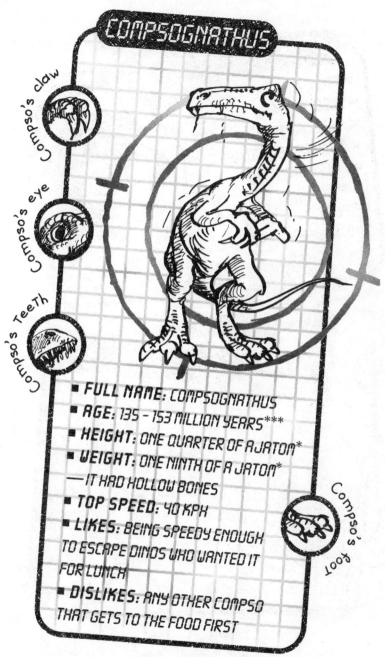

COMPSOGNATHUS

Compso's claw

Compso's eye

Compso's teeth

Compso's foot

- **FULL NAME:** COMPSOGNATHUS
- **AGE:** 135 – 153 MILLION YEARS***
- **HEIGHT:** ONE QUARTER OF A JATOM*
- **WEIGHT:** ONE NINTH OF A JATOM*
  —IT HAD HOLLOW BONES
- **TOP SPEED:** 40 KPH
- **LIKES:** BEING SPEEDY ENOUGH TO ESCAPE DINOS WHO WANTED IT FOR LUNCH
- **DISLIKES:** ANY OTHER COMPSO THAT GETS TO THE FOOD FIRST

*NOTE: A JATOM IS THE SIZE OF JAMIE OR TOM: 125 CM TALL AND 27 KG IN WEIGHT
***NOTE: SCIENTISTS CALL THIS PERIOD THE JURASSIC

DINOSAUR COVE

Village

Marina

Sealight Head

Landslips where clay and fossils are

Muddy beach

DINO CAVE

High Tide beach line

Low Tide beach line

Sea

Smuggler's Point

The dinosaur museum was alive with dinosaurs—
tiny T-Rex, a small pack of diplodocuses, grounded
miniature pterodactyls, and a velociraptor arguing
with a stegosaurus over who had the better
costume. Jamie Morgan and his best friend Tom
Clay were herding them all into the activity room.

'I've never seen so many people here,' said
Jamie.

Tom laughed as a little triceratops with
lopsided horns raced by. 'Dress as a Dino Day
was a great idea of your dad's.'

The two boys squeezed in at the back of the room as the children watched Jamie's dad show film clips about the Jurassic Age. Computer-generated stegosaurs lumbered across the screen; then a herd of allosaurs attacked a huge diplodocus.

'Now,' said Dad. 'Let's look at the landscape. It's just as exciting.'

The film showed a picture of a huge land mass. 'This is Pangaea,' he told his round-eyed audience. 'There were no separate continents in the world like there are today—just this lump of land. But that was about to change.'

Pangaea
(before volcanoes
and earthquakes)

Pangaea
(after volcanoes
and earthquakes)

BOOM!

An erupting volcano appeared on the screen.
Shrieks of delight filled the room.

'The volcanoes and earthquakes broke
up Pangaea like a jigsaw puzzle,' said Jamie's
dad. 'That was the start of the continents
we know now.'

'And now it's time for lunch!' Jamie's dad
announced. 'There are sandwiches and crisps
at the back, so if you get in line . . .'

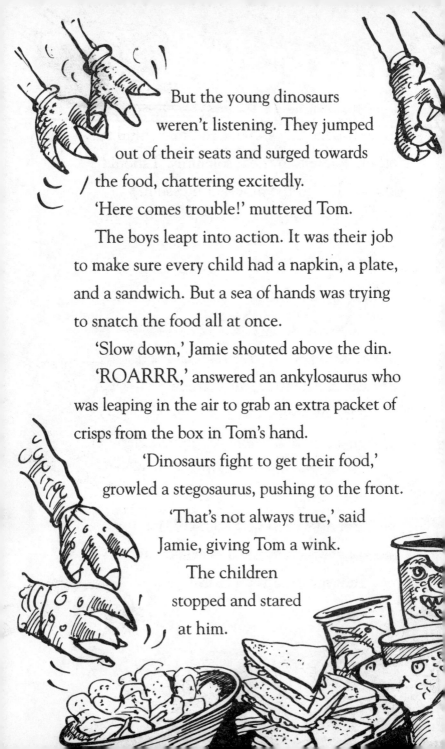

But the young dinosaurs weren't listening. They jumped out of their seats and surged towards the food, chattering excitedly.

'Here comes trouble!' muttered Tom.

The boys leapt into action. It was their job to make sure every child had a napkin, a plate, and a sandwich. But a sea of hands was trying to snatch the food all at once.

'Slow down,' Jamie shouted above the din.

'ROARRR,' answered an ankylosaurus who was leaping in the air to grab an extra packet of crisps from the box in Tom's hand.

'Dinosaurs fight to get their food,' growled a stegosaurus, pushing to the front.

'That's not always true,' said Jamie, giving Tom a wink.

The children stopped and stared at him.

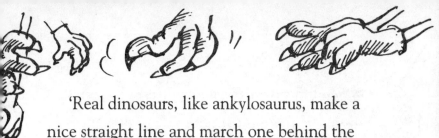

'Real dinosaurs, like ankylosaurus, make a nice straight line and march one behind the other,' Jamie told them solemnly. 'I should know. I live in the dinosaur museum.'

The dinosaurs immediately shuffled into a line, arms—and wings—by their sides.

'That was brilliant!' Tom whispered to Jamie as he poured juice into dinosaur cups. 'I thought we were going to be trampled.'

Soon all the children had marched off, with some very realistic roaring, to eat their lunch.

Jamie stared at the image that was still on the screen—the huge mountain ranges of the Jurassic era.

'No wonder the kids got excited,' he said, taking a handful of crisps.

'That presentation of Dad's was awesome.'

'Should we check out some real Jurassic mountains?' Tom whispered.

'Good idea,' Jamie agreed. 'We haven't explored the mountains in Dino World yet.'

The boys had a secret. Deep in the cliffs of Dinosaur Cove, they had found the entrance to a magical world of living dinosaurs. They went there whenever they could.

Jamie grinned. 'We've helped with lunch like we promised . . . '

At that moment Jamie's dad rushed past. 'Forgot to tell them to wash their hands before they hit the museum!'

'We're just going out for a bit,' Jamie told him.

'OK, see you later!' Dad was gone.

Jamie checked in his backpack. Everything was there: the Fossil Finder, notebook, and Jurassic ammonite to take them into the right dino time. He swung it onto his back.

Tom snatched up some ham sandwiches. 'We'll need lunch too,' he said, tucking them into the backpack.

As they left, they passed Grandad trying to stop a triceratops feeding crisps to the edmontosaurus skeleton.

The boys scrambled up the dry stream bed that led to the secret smugglers' cave and then began to climb the boulders. Jamie reached for a handhold to pull himself over a ledge.

KERACK!

The rock split off in his hand and he lost his grip. Jamie was dangling by only one arm high above the ground!

Tom shot out a hand and grasped Jamie's arm in a firm grip.

'Thanks!' breathed Jamie, scrambling for safety as loose rock and pebbles rattled away down the boulders. 'One rock cracks and I nearly fall down the cliff. Imagine what it must have been like when the whole of Pangaea split apart!'

Climbing more carefully now, the boys pulled themselves up to the smugglers' cave and into the secret chamber.

'There are Wanna's footprints, waiting for us,' said Jamie, placing his trainers in the shallow dips on the stony floor. He felt the usual bubble of excitement as they followed the line of prints to the cave wall and . . .

A blast of hot air hit their faces and they found themselves stepping out of Gingko Cave amongst the giant trees of Jurassic Dino World.

'Phwah!' panted Tom, wiping his forehead. 'It's steamier than ever.'

'The trees are dripping with water,' said Jamie. 'Looks like we've just missed a rainstorm.'

Flickers of sunlight were breaking through the leaves of the huge trees above and drops of water plopped down on their heads. Suddenly the boys heard a rustling sound from the horsehair ferns in front of them. Spray flew up and soaked them as a dripping wet, green and brown dinosaur charged out of the undergrowth and skidded to a halt at their feet.

'Wanna!' exclaimed Jamie, wiping his face. 'Thanks for the shower.'

'Want to come mountaineering with us?' Tom asked, giving their dinosaur friend a scratch on his flat, bony head.

Grunk!

'I think that's a yes!' Jamie laughed as Wanna ran round in excited circles.

'The Misty Mountains are to the north.' Tom checked his compass. 'This way.'

They soon reached the edge of the stifling jungle. Ahead, the flat plains steamed in the heat and beyond rose the high peaks of the cone-like mountains, purple against the sky.

'They're awesome,' said Jamie. 'And look at those dark clouds above them. I bet there's another storm coming.'

'I think the dinosaurs have sensed it,'
agreed Tom, peering intently through his
binoculars. 'There's hardly a sniff of life on
the plains today.'

'What are we waiting for?' said Jamie.
'We don't want to get caught in the open by
a prehistoric downpour.'

They set off at a sprint across the plains,
splashing through the puddles left by the rain.
Wanna galloped ahead. At last they reached
the green lower slopes of the Misty Mountains.

Jamie gazed up at the dark,
rugged peaks towering above them,
disappearing in the clouds. 'What a
sight!' he breathed.

Grunk! The little dinosaur
stopped and looked up as if puzzled.
'Yes, that's where we're heading,
Wanna,' said Tom.

They started climbing through thick
ferns, disturbing huge, brightly-coloured insects
as they went. But Wanna hung back.

'Come on, boy,' called Jamie. 'It's
just getting a bit steep. You'll be OK.'

24

The little dinosaur hesitated for a moment then he trotted along behind them, staying close to their heels. Soon the vegetation stopped, and they were clambering up the bare rocks alongside a pebbly stream. Wanna poked his head in and drank with huge slurping noises.

Jamie stopped and looked back to where the Massive Canyon ran across the plains down to the ocean. 'The water's heading for the canyon,' he said.

'Today history is being made,' announced Tom into an imaginary microphone. 'Our intrepid Jurassic trio are exploring the Misty Mountains. They are the only humans—and wannanosaurus—ever to attempt such a climb. Steam is rising from the mountainside as rainwater evaporates. What will they find? Does anything live in this strange place?'

EEK, EEK!

A shrill squawk filled the air. The boys froze.

A beaky brown nose poked out from the
steaming ferns. Then a whole head appeared,
with little bright eyes that swivelled this
way and that, checking the area. Finally a
strange creature, no bigger than a chicken,
stalked out and shook itself. It took no notice
of the two boys but scuttled away on stiff
back legs towards the stream bed. Jamie and
Tom snorted with laughter as its head darted
down to drink and its tail bobbed up in
the air.

Wanna cocked his head on one side. He looked puzzled.

'Have you ever seen anything so funny?' said Jamie, laughing.

'It walks like a cartoon dinosaur!' Tom spluttered. 'I've seen it in books but it's a lot funnier in real life.'

'It's a compsognathus,' said Jamie. 'But I don't know much about them.' He opened his Fossil Finder. *'PRONOUNCED KOMP-SOG-NA-THUS WHICH MEANS "PRETTY JAW".'*

'I wouldn't call that pretty!' Tom scoffed. 'What else does it say?'

'SPEEDY TWO-LEGGED CARNIVORE,' Jamie read on. *'ONE OF THE SMALLEST DINOSAURS.'*

Another beaky head popped out of the ferns. 'Looks like it's got a friend,' said Tom.

Squawking, the newcomer scuttled over to the water. 'Wonder what they'll do if we go up to them.'

Tom began to climb over a rock to get to the drinking dinosaurs. But his foot slipped on some loose stones. 'Yaieee!' he yelped as he stumbled. Immediately the two heads shot up and two pairs of beady eyes studied Tom.

Yaieee! Yaieee! the creatures called back.

'Wow!' Jamie said as he hauled Tom to his feet. 'They're copying you.'

Tom made the noise again. This time four more heads appeared and all the compsos joined in with the sound. Soon the calls of the mimicking creatures were bouncing off the rocks.

'You know how experts think some dinosaurs evolved into birds,' said Tom. 'I reckon these compsos became parrots!'

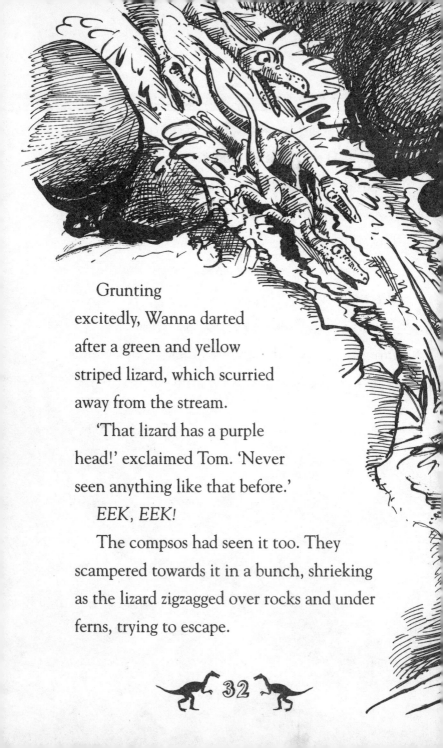

Grunting excitedly, Wanna darted after a green and yellow striped lizard, which scurried away from the stream.

'That lizard has a purple head!' exclaimed Tom. 'Never seen anything like that before.'

EEK, EEK!

The compsos had seen it too. They scampered towards it in a bunch, shrieking as the lizard zigzagged over rocks and under ferns, trying to escape.

'That lizard had better watch out,' said
Jamie, 'or he's going to be compso lunch!'
Wanna was left behind as the eager little
creatures raced along after it.

'And the compsognathuses are gaining on
their prey,' announced Tom into his pretend
microphone. 'More have appeared. They're
fighting over it . . . can you hear those angry
chatterings? I think it's going to get away . . .
No, the smallest compso has caught
it and now all the others
are after him.'

The little compso dashed past, lizard tail dangling from its mouth, pursued by the others. Jamie laughed. 'They remind me of the kids at the museum—obsessed with food.'

'And you told them that dinosaurs make an orderly queue,' said Tom. 'I'm glad they can't see what really happens.'

The compso gulped the lizard down and the chase ended. The rest of the bunch began sniffing around, looking for more food. Then one strutted eagerly towards the boys.

'Look out,' said Jamie. 'We've got company.'

'It looks like a mini ostrich,' said Tom, as the little creature stalked round them, neck outstretched, sniffing their scent.

'It's very friendly,' said Jamie. 'And quite cute
. . . Aah!' He leapt in alarm as the dinosaur
suddenly jumped onto his back with a screech.
'Help!' he yelled. 'Its claws are digging right in.'

The determined compso started scratching
at the top of Jamie's backpack.

'It's after the sandwiches,' called Tom. 'Oh
no you don't, you little thief.' He grabbed the
bird-like dinosaur round its waist and tugged.
But it was surprisingly strong and clung on
with its long claws. Jamie's arms flailed
about as he tried to knock
the creature off and Wanna
grunked anxiously
around their feet.

At last Tom gave a great tug, pulling the backpack right off Jamie's back. The compso let go as the backpack crashed to the ground. Tom grabbed the pack as the determined dinosaur looked the boys up and down, searching for a way to get its snack.

Wanna grunked crossly at it, then waddled away up the steep mountainside.

'Good thinking, Wanna,' said Tom, putting the backpack onto his shoulders as Jamie rubbed at the scratches the little creature had left on him. 'Let's go before any more get the idea that we're a tuck shop.'

'Agreed,' said Jamie grimly. 'Those compsos are not as cute as I thought.'

They set off after Wanna but soon found themselves surrounded by a crowd of chattering dinosaurs. Compsos darted out of the ferns and leapt at them from every rock and stone.

'Uh oh!' whispered Jamie. 'We're in big trouble now.'

EEK,

EEK!

The little creatures jostled against the boys, pecking and scratching at their legs.

'We can't make a run for it,' said Tom, looking around at the carpet of chirping dinosaurs. 'There's nowhere to put our feet.'

'They *are* just like the pesky kids at the museum,' said Jamie. 'And that's given me an idea.' He reached into the backpack on Tom's shoulders, pulled out a sandwich and

waved it at the creatures. When he had
their attention, he tossed it into the ferns.
The compsos were on it like a swarm of bees.

'Well done,' said Tom. 'Let's get away from
here while they're busy fighting for it.'

'Too late,' groaned Jamie. 'They're coming
back for more. Ouch!'

The hungry little compsognathuses were back, raking their sharp claws against the boys' knees.

'They don't mean any harm,' said Tom, trying to push them away, 'but they're hurting.'

Grunk, GRUNK!

Wanna was back, running around the crowd, trying to get to the boys.

'Yow!' Tom was suddenly pulled sideways.
'What's going on?'

'One of them has got the backpack strap,'
called Jamie. 'They want more sandwiches.'

The hungry dinosaur gave a tug. Tom
staggered as he tried to wrench the strap away.
But now compsos from all around were
joining in the tug of war and Tom was no
match for them.

'Help!' he cried as he lost his balance and
crashed to the ground. Soon he was covered
in chirping dinosaurs all searching
for food.

Gerunk! Wanna came to his rescue.
He butted and pushed the little creatures
away. Jamie saw his chance. He grabbed
Tom's arm and pulled him to his feet.

'Thanks . . . both of you . . . ' Tom was out
of breath.

'How are we going to escape?' Jamie
wondered. 'They're everywhere.'

'Let's try the ham decoy again,' said Tom,
taking Jamie's backpack off and reaching
into it. 'I'll try and throw the sandwich a bit

further this time.' He lobbed it deep into the nearby ferns.

Some of the compsos scampered off and started hunting for it.

'Run!' shouted Jamie, grabbing his backpack. 'While we've got the chance.'

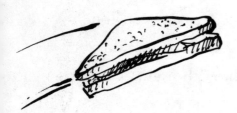

But the other compsos weren't so easily fooled. They chased after the boys.

'Let's jump in the stream,' yelled Tom. 'Maybe they don't like getting wet.'

They splashed into the shallow water that trickled down from the mountain.

'It's working!' said Jamie, looking over his shoulder. 'They've stopped.'

The compsos were leaping about on the bank, squeaking and chattering crossly, but they didn't follow.

Tom, Jamie, and Wanna splashed upstream. Soon they had left the annoying

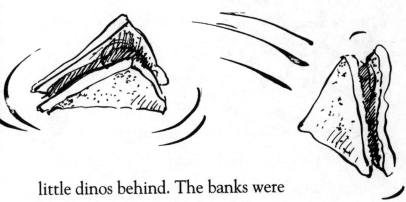

little dinos behind. The banks were becoming higher as they climbed.

'Hey! Have you noticed something strange?' said Tom. 'The water's warm—really warm.'

'You're right,' agreed Jamie. 'Even though it's ice melted from the top of the mountain.' He peered up the stream bed. 'It's much steeper now.'

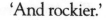

'And rockier.'

Tom looked down at the jagged stones beneath their feet. 'See the way the rock has little holes in it? That means it's an igneous rock.'

'I remember Dad telling us about that,' agreed Jamie. 'Igneous rocks are made from magma.'

'And magma is the hot molten rock inside the Earth,' said Tom.

'Which only comes up when a volcano erupts,' added Jamie.

'And then it's called lava!' exclaimed Tom.

They looked at each other.

'That means . . . ' began Jamie.

'Misty Mountain isn't just a mountain . . . ' said Tom.

'It's a dormant volcano,' finished Jamie. 'Awesome!'

'I'd love to have seen it erupt,' said Tom, his eyes shining. 'There would have been rumbling and shaking and rivers of lava streaming down.'

'Let's see if we can make it to the crater at the top,' said Jamie.

They scrambled over boulders, trainers slipping on the wet ground. Wanna kept close behind.

'Phwah!' gasped Jamie. 'Can you smell that?'

Tom flapped his hand in front of his face. 'It's like rotten eggs,' he said. 'Worse than gingko.'

'What is it?' Jamie was holding his nose now.

GRUNK!

Wanna stopped. He was trembling with fright, his eyes wild.

GRUNK, GRUNK!

'What's the matter, boy?' asked Jamie.

'Something's really bothering him.' Wanna
dashed down the volcano and the boys
hurried after him, worried.

Then the ground beneath them began
to shake.

RUMMMMMBLE!

'Feels like an earthquake,' cried Jamie,
staggering on the shuddering rock. 'Wanna
must have sensed it before we did.'

'Help!' The boys went sprawling
on the stones. Wanna only kept
his balance by spreading all
four paws out wide.

The shaking stopped as suddenly as it had started.

Jamie jumped to his feet. 'Yow!' he exclaimed. 'The ground's really hot.'

'Hot ground, steamy rainwater, thick mist, strangely quiet plains.' Tom looked over at Jamie in horror. 'Uh oh.'

'This volcano isn't dormant at all,' said Jamie. 'It's active, and it's going to erupt!'

GARUMMBBLE!

The earth shook again, harder this time.

KABOOM!

The sound of a deafening explosion split the air and a massive cloud of black smoke blasted up from the volcano. Bright orange lava bubbled from the top. It poured over the side in a fast flowing river.

'Look out!' cried Tom. 'It's heading straight for us!'

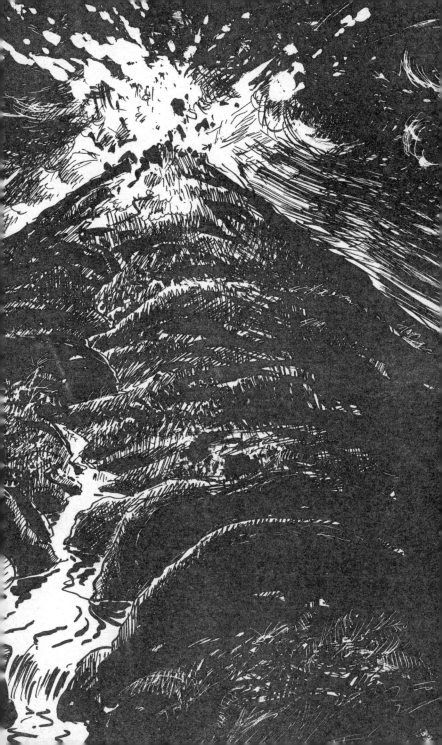

CHAPTER 5

'Run!' shouted Jamie.

The lava flow was fast, very fast. The boys
turned and scrambled down between the
steep banks of the stream bed. Wanna sent
up a cloud of spray as he charged ahead.

Tom looked back over his shoulder. 'We've
got to get out of this stream bed,' he yelled
desperately. 'The lava's using it as a channel.
And it's travelling much faster than we are.'

Jamie could see what he meant. The
molten orange lava was taking the quickest

route to get down the volcano—and they
were right in its path.

Spitting and crackling, it surged
towards them. Jamie started to haul
himself up the slippery bank.

GRUNK! GRUNK!

Jamie looked back.
Wanna was trying in vain
to climb out after them!

'Quick, Wanna!'
yelled Jamie.

'We have to help him,'
shouted Tom, above the
roar of the lava.

They flattened
themselves on the bank,
and Jamie could feel the heat
of the approaching lava burning
his arms. The boys grabbed a paw
each and heaved Wanna to safety.

55

'Just in time!' said
Tom, wiping the sweat
from his forehead.

Wanna cowered behind them,
watching the hot, spluttering flow
bubble past down the volcano. Rocks
popped with heat as they were
engulfed in the boiling mass.

The boys backed away, shielding their
eyes from the glare.

'I've never felt anything so hot,' said Jamie.

'We need to get to the plains,' urged Tom. 'It's not safe here.'

They skidded down the steep slope, jumping over rocks and finally pushing through ferns near the bottom until they ran out of breath.

Jamie took a quick glance back and saw that the lava stream hadn't reached as far as the green lower slopes. 'Hey,' he panted. 'The lava has stopped!'

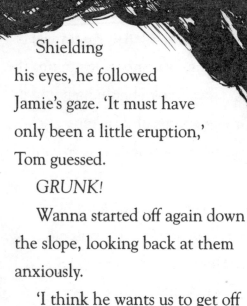

Shielding his eyes, he followed Jamie's gaze. 'It must have only been a little eruption,' Tom guessed.

GRUNK!

Wanna started off again down the slope, looking back at them anxiously.

'I think he wants us to get off the mountain,' said Jamie.

BOOM!

The boys ducked down, covering their ears, as another deafening explosion filled the air.

'Oh no!' cried Tom, pointing to the top of the volcano. 'I think that was just the beginning!'

A huge tongue of fire was shooting up into the sky. Smoke blasted out and a great surge of lava began to tumble out from the crater, rapidly covering the bare rock.

'There's oceans of the stuff!' Jamie shouted. 'It's spilling out everywhere.'

The boys didn't wait to see any more. They hurtled down the slippery slope, Wanna leading the way.

Rounding a dense clump of ferns they suddenly found themselves surrounded by lizards and insects swarming about in panic. And the silly group of compsognathuses were squawking around, feasting on the fleeing creatures.

'I don't believe it!'
exclaimed Tom, trying not
to crush anything underfoot.

'They don't seem to realize the
volcano's spilling its guts,' Jamie said.
'They're just after snacks!'

Tom and Jamie looked at each other. 'They're
going to get fried,' said Tom, with horror.

'We have to make them move,' Jamie decided.

Tom waved his arms and ran at the compsos.
They ignored him and carried on snacking,
chirping happily as they went.

'What are we going to do?'
Jamie looked round for an answer.
The lava had reached the top of the
vegetation. Bushes and ferns disappeared,
burnt to ashes as they were engulfed by the
rolling wall of molten rock.

'Got an idea,' shouted Tom.

He ran among the compsognathuses,
letting out a loud, YAIEE!

The little dinosaurs stopped
and looked at him, open-mouthed.
Tom squawked again. *YAIEE!*

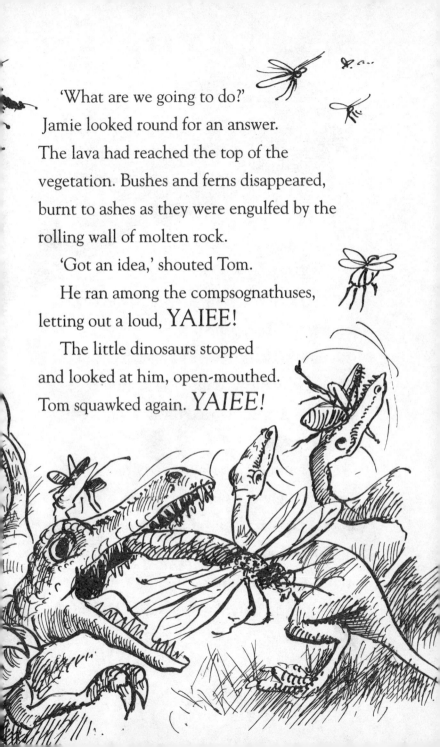

The compsos copied him.

YAIEE! YAIEE!

'Now I've got their attention, show them some food,' Tom yelled.

Jamie pulled another sandwich out of the backpack. He waved it at the compsos. They smelt the ham and raced towards him, eyes shining greedily.

'Let's lure them away,' cried Tom.

Jamie held the sandwich above his head and the boys started to run down the mountain again. The band of greedy compsos scampered after them.

'Got to go faster,' yelled Tom. 'The lava's getting closer.'

YAIEE!

The boys pounded along as fast as they
could. Jamie wondered how long he could
keep up the pace. His heart was racing and his
legs were hurting with every step. And he
knew that the compsos couldn't run for as
long as he could. The lava was rolling down
in a sheet of searing orange heat—gaining on
them with every second.

They were all going to be swallowed up.

With gasping breaths Jamie and Tom crashed on through the ferns, Wanna in the lead and the compsos behind. Jamie could feel his heart almost bursting from his chest as he waited for the molten lava to surge over him.

But nothing happened. At last he couldn't bear it any longer. He threw a terrified glance over his shoulder. He expected to see a wall of bubbling lava about to crash down on him like a huge wave. But there was nothing there. Wiping the sweat from his eyes, he peered up

the slope. High above, the lava was pouring into a new stream bed. It had found a quicker way down the mountain.

He bent double, trying to catch his breath. 'We can stop!' he yelled to Tom. 'The flow is heading away. Towards Massive Canyon.'

'What a relief!' Tom punched the air. 'The canyon's deep enough to take all that lava.'

'That means Jurassic Dino World is safe, and so are the compsos,' added Jamie as a bunch of the little creatures caught up with them. Soon the boys were surrounded by a sea of squawking dinosaurs, jumping for the sandwich that was still in Jamie's hand.

'Jump all you like!' Tom told them, laughing. 'We're just glad you didn't get covered in lava.'

Wanna ran around crossly head-butting the excited compsos away, but they ignored him and kept clamouring at the boys.

'This'll sort them out,' called Jamie. He broke the sandwich into small pieces, keeping it high above their heads. Then he threw the pieces in different directions.

All the compsognathuses heads looked this way and that—and in an instant they scattered after the shower of food, squawking at the tops of their voices. The fastest ones swept the pieces up in their teeth and the rest gave chase with their funny stiff-legged run.

'We've had an awesome adventure!' said Jamie, brushing volcanic dust out of his hair.

'Escape from the Jurassic volcano,' announced Tom. 'It would make a great TV programme.'

'Time to head home,' said Jamie, turning towards Gingko Cave. 'To see how Dad's got on with *his* greedy dinosaurs.'

They stopped at the edge of the jungle to take one last look at the Misty Mountains with the thick plume of smoke still rising from its crater.

Tom breathed a sigh of relief. 'The lava flow has stopped now.'

'There's a herd of brachiosaurs in the distance,' said Jamie, pointing. 'And some diplodocuses nibbling at those trees over there.'

'The dinosaurs are all coming back to the Plains,' said Tom. 'They must know the danger's over.'

'Everything is back to normal then,' said Jamie.

'Well,' said Tom, 'normal for our Jurassic World. And that's . . .'

'AWESOME!' they shouted together.

'Can't wait till next time,' said Jamie.

They plunged through the giant trees and splashed through a little river to get some of the volcanic dust off. Soon they had reached Gingko Cave.

Tom picked Wanna three
juicy gingkoes from a nearby
tree. 'Those greedy compsos
shouldn't have all the
fun, boy,' he said as
he tossed them to
their little dinosaur friend.

Wanna stuffed them all in his mouth at
once and settled down to chomp. The boys
waved goodbye, placed their feet into the
dino footprints and walked backwards into
their own world.

As Jamie and Tom walked down the
path to the beach, they heard shouts and
cheers from below. A crowd of dinosaurs
was waving and beckoning at them. Dad
and Grandad were standing in the middle,
looking frazzled.

'Don't think we'll be able to escape this lot,'
said Jamie as the boys headed along the beach.

Dad ran up. 'Thank goodness you're here!' he said. 'We're having a football match— carnivores versus herbivores. Will you referee?'

Grandad threw the ball to Jamie and the whistle to Tom. Jamie quickly placed the ball down on the sand for kick off and Tom blew the whistle to start the game.

In an instant every single footballer was charging towards them! Tom and Jamie were soon buried under a pile of cheering dinosaurs. At last a small pterodactyl got

possession of the ball
and all the others headed
off after it, with a lot
of prehistoric
shrieking.

Jamie and Tom
sat up and watched
the eager herd make
for the goal.

Tom grinned.
'I wonder who'd win
if they played the compsognathuses!'

'I know one thing,' answered Jamie.
'I wouldn't want to be the referee for
that match!'

DINOSAUR WORLD

----- BOYS' ROUTE

Humongous
Waterfall

Massive Canyon

Plains

Fin Rock

Jurassic
Ocean

Misty Mountains

Thick Jungle

Gingko Cave

Discovery Hills

GLOSSARY

Brachiosaurus (bra-kee-oh-sor-us) – had a long neck, like a giraffe. This gentle giant loved its greens, munching through 200 kg of plants a day!

Compsognathus (komp-sog-nay-thus) – a turkey-sized dinosaur that walked on two legs. The first dinosaur found with a reasonably complete skeleton, but not the smallest dinosaur as originally thought.

Diplodocus (dip-lod-oh-kus) – one of the longest land dinosaurs with a long-neck and whip-like tail. This huge dinosaur had pencil-shaped blunt teeth perfect for its plant-only diet.

Dormant – as if in a deep sleep or, in the case of a volcano, temporarily inactive.

Igneous rock (ig-nee-us) – rock formed by the solidification of magma or lava.

Jurassic – from about 150 to 200 million years ago, the Jurassic age was warm and humid, with lush jungle cover and great marine diversity. Large dinosaurs ruled on land, while the first birds took to the air.

Pangaea (pan-gee-ah) – a single continent that existed about 250 million years ago before the continents were separated into their current configuration.

Lava – very hot rock spewed out by a volcano during an eruption.

Magma – fluid or semi-fluid material within the earth's crust from which lava and other igneous rock is formed by cooling.

Molten – a solid liquefied by heat.

Wannanosaurus (wah-nan-oh-sor-us) – a dinosaur that only ate plants and used its hard, flat skull to defend itself. Named after the place it was discovered: Wannano in China.

Catch me
if you can!
I'm coming next …